SIX WORD WONDER

OVER FIVE HUNDRED ORIGINAL SIX WORD
STORIES, JOKES AND POEMS TO ENTERTAIN
AND AMUSE

DOUG WELLER

ABOUT THE AUTHOR

Doug Weller is an emerging writer of thrillers, and the brain behind the Six Word Wonder.

This is Doug's second book.

facebook.com/sixwordwonder

twitter.com/realdougweller

instagram.com/sixwordwonder

Six Word Wonder by Doug Weller

First printing: May 2020

Published by Hebe Publications

Some characters and events in this book are fictitious. Any similarity to real persons, living or dead, is coincidental and not intended by the author.

ISBN: 9798646177262

ASIN: B089CH5ZZ9

Visit: www.dougweller.net

Brevity is the soul of wit

William Shakespeare

This book is dedicated to words.

Six words to tell a story.
Not three or eight or twenty.
You may ask - is six enough?
Well, trust me, six is plenty.

Small, tall tales to entice you,
Some poetic, some cruel, some funny.
Joy and twists, horror and pain,
And some that tickle your tummy.

Devour them all in one sitting,
Or carefully sip them like wine.
With each of us endlessly busy,
Brief tales will unlock your time.

Hemingway made much of the mini,
Chewed words up like buttered sweetcorn.
Allegedly, drunk, one night, he typed:
'For Sale: Baby Shoes. Never worn.'

But now, let's finish this intro,
We've established your dislike of waste.
My hope? These six word wonders,
will give you a nourishing taste.

1

THE FIRST MOVEMENT

Born a pawn.
Died a queen.

———

Dragon slain.
Damsel rescued.
Still bored.

———

Me,
became we,
became a family.

———

His first breath.
Her last breath.

―――――

'Tis the season for nuclear winter.

―――――

At arrivals. Flowers in hand. Waiting.

―――――

Desired.
Hired.
Eventually tired,
then retired.

―――――

He's a priest! Not a criminal...

―――――

Hearse arrives outside.
'Your ride, Madam.'

―――――

Loved you until you said,
'Pacifically.'

…mind. Gifted Mediums can read your…

Romance wasn't dead.
But he was.

Single.
Mingled.
Laughed.
Loved.
Lied.
Alone.

Unlocking the cage,
she stepped out.

Honestly,
I accidentally sat on it.

Voice of angel.
Face of snail.

Rejoice!
The bees have taken charge.

The lump grows silently within me.

Under the makeup,
she was beautiful.

Love conquers all.
Except my piles.

Fast food.
Fast cars.
Fast death.

―――――

God creates snooze button,
then rests.

―――――

He forgot he had dementia. Daily.

―――――

Nose ran
at the feet's smell.

―――――

Woke in bed.
A flower bed.

―――――

You undress. I make a mess.

―――――

The devil became…
a geography teacher.

Scissors killed paper,
beaten by rock.

Procrastinator finally finished something.
His life.

The sharpest thorns didn't save Rose.

Blood on hands. Yours and mine.

Urgent Flatshare:
Professionals only.
Exorcist preferred.

'I demand respect.'
'I supply contempt.'

Ear in envelope.
Now he'd listen.

As we baited, the sharks waited.

At work,
she blinked.
Everybody died!

Classmate copied my homework.
Now missing.

For sale: Ski boots.
Wanted: Wheelchair.

Beauty's skin deep?
Let's find out…

First, we spooned.
Then, we forked.

Serial cheater swiped right.
She left.

He undressed her, then raised scalpel.

The wicked stepmother
was
kinda hot.

These were his last six words…

2
_____

DOING A JOB IN SIX WORDS

The hazards of working are many.
Here we explore just a few.
Some of us like to forget work,
Others just hide in the loo.

Auditor was ticked
and then bashed.

At the wedding,
the photographer snapped.

So, you're that blood-sucking phlebotomist.

Terminated fireman:
Fought fire with fire.

Lion tamer couldn't tame his kids.

Yesterday, they dug up an archeologist.

Yoga teacher.
Bent out of shape.

Air traffic controller's last day?
Impactful.

Statistician miscalculated his chance of survival.

Ambitious actuary never drew his pension.

Acute Nurse
became Tinder sensation.

Designer found,
hung by fashionable tie.

Composer's suicide note found -
B flat.

Astrologer's star sign,
ironically,
was cancer.

3

THE SECOND MOVEMENT

Cinderella trades
glass slippers
for shotgun.

Ambulance finally arrived.
Left without siren.

Beneath the stars,
they finally kissed.

Forgotten what I was going to…

Autocorrect fixed all of my worms.

Broke promise.
Broke down.
Broke up.

Discovered antidote to love.
Earned billions.

I kissed her neck,
then pushed.

Astronomer waited until sunrise
for revenge.

Bed springs creak above my head.

First, they automated all the politicians.

Hand on her face wasn't his.

Trusted.
Devoted.
Loved.
Then inevitably betrayed.

Looked up from basket to guillotine.

My ice cream drips.
I scream.

If Grandaddy's dead…
…why's he outside?

In another dimension,
we just met.

Humpty Dumpty:
Not a bad egg.

In bed,
the zoologist's an animal.

Juicy Lucy played with her uzi.

Knew the ropes.
Forgot the knots.

Asian relocated for job.
Korea change.

Last night,
he tried on heels.

Old dog.
New tricks.
Surprisingly, juggling.

Party dress. Melted into her skin.

Saw a Blur, not an Oasis.

You're the world president…
Now what?

Special order made for Chubby's coffin.

Positive this is vegan? It's mooing.

That day, the sun didn't set.

The Visitors classified me under food.

Unicorn?
Just a well-groomed rhinoceros.

The lightest touch.
The heaviest pain.

James Joyce checked his Amazon ranking

The wounded animal deserved every kick.

Salt water
tasted
like warm air.

Your presence means my continued absence.

Mangy rug's past life?
Magic carpet.

Knuckles dragging.
Chests out.
Skulls empty.

Waited until Valentine's
to say goodbye.

Watched TV every day.
Died happy.

Duckling returned after winter.
Still ugly.

We both came
before she left.

Wrapped in foil.
Ready for pot.

Kept the scars when you left.

You may now kiss
the bridesmaid.

Zombies infest streets, demanding equal rights.

The syringe emptied.
Her body slumped.

Told a joke. Forgot the punch...

We never got to say goodbye.

WORLD HISTORY: SUMMED UP IN SIXES

The world seems a complex place,
Filled with drama, light and pain,
Six words can't detail every blip,
But can capture the essence again.

Appeasement failed.
Bomb dropped.
Peace restored.

Painted sunflowers.
Severed ear.
Died alone.

Casting couch.
Stray hands.
Life imprisonment.

In a french tunnel, Di died.

It's a baby boy, Frau Hitler.

First rules.
Then uniforms.
Then guns.

———

Alexa's life was perfect…
until 2014.

———

Tasted the apple…
then got naked!

———

Ted.
Underestimated.
Celebrated.
Elevated.
Venerated.
Assassinated.

———

Thousands left the trenches.
Few returned.

———

'Unbelievable. Tutankhamun!'
'Friends call me Toots.'

Disowned princess lived happily never after.

Normandy landings.
Got lucky.
Liberated France.

Before 1066,
he was plain Will.

Set aside and ostracised.
Radicalised.
Genocide.

Welcome to the dark ages. Again…

5

THE THIRD MOVEMENT

Born.
Preached.
Inspired.
Betrayed.
Crucified.
Resurrected.

Leave Grandma's ashes in the ashtray.

War, Iron, Cheese. All the mongers.

God checks manual.
Orders a reboot.

Created unbreakable new password... forgot it.

Schrodinger's cat
got impatient.
Killed herself.

God visited on Sunday.
'Everything's closed!'

For sale: Love letters. Never opened.

The telegram read,
'She's still married.'

Tonight involves fun, and a gun.

That jellyfish just called ME spineless!

Some books are like tortoises. Hardbacks.

The virus spread,
until we're dead.

Supercilious archaeologist
became a living fossil.

Unknown writer.
Never read.
Kept writing.

Found: Technicolor dreamcoat.
Covered in blood.

Protagonist dead.
Villain triumphs.
Sidekick conflicted.

She's half-human,
and half-vegan.

Forget Santa.
Just believe in yourself.

Dirty nails.
Unwashed hair.
Owns Ferrari...

Awkward!
Billie Jean was my lover.

He took a memento.
Her heart.

Tasty mint sauce silenced the lambs

Pure imagination.
But really filthy reality

The whole world knew,
except you.

Shared dreams.
Shared lies.
Shared goodbyes.

Mail arrived from tax authority… Puppies!!!

If rest is rust,
I'm dust.

The perfect pupil taught the teacher.

Discovered your true passion?
Do that.

Only wisdom I've got is teeth.

Test results?
Negative… As in bad.

Today, ended a seriously bleak week.

'So *you're* his boyfriend,' mumbled girlfriend.

———

Tunnel's complete.
Your cell or mine?

———

'Your sister's DNA's normal.'
'My wife's???'

———

Contradicting him,
Supposedly determined,
Her execution.

———

Ace.
King.
Queen.
Jack.
Bluff.
Damn.

———

Attempted sobriety. Drove me to drink.

Back then, he called it tickling…

Eloquence,
Multiplied by ambition,
Minus humanity.

First visitors in weeks were maggots.

Hugged her 'til her bones cracked.

My superhuman skill is gargle singing.

Home alone, but toilet just flushed…

6

WORD GAMES IN SIX WORD FORM

Below; haikus, palindromes, acrostics and rebus.
Enjoy puzzling your way slowly through.
If you dislike, blame the author,
No doubt, the author blames you.

Man wanted it. It wanted man.

My satisfaction,
Minuscule literature,
Creative haiku.

An ax
to do
my ox.

'U C A B?'
'I C.'

Race horse had had horse race.

…ended. The day started as it…

You came
between
tea and Vee.

After
Dinner,
Usually
Like
To
Sleep

Richard *told* you, you told Richard.

My
Only
Nightmare,
Dream
About
Yesterday

'R U O K, J?'
'Y?'

One day,
she say
she gay.

Pour
four
more
'till
head
sore.

You complete me, said the emu.

The cow heard the cow herd.

7

THE FOURTH MOVEMENT

In my dreams, you're still here.

Horror?
Knowing someone
is following you.

Broken promises.
Broken hearts.
Broken home.

Baby loves whining. Mummy loves wine.

He only got to cry once…

Everything she touched turned to asshole.

Hook.
Catalyst.
Complications.
Hopelessness.
Climax.
Denouement

In one unique explosion: the universe.

Won a million.
Lost her mind.

He optimised his shortcuts… Still lonely.

Regained consciousness.
Need new dental records.

To do:
Eat,
Regret,
Vomit,
Repeat.

Old MacDonald had a locust infestation.

One bite, and her reflection vanished.

President couldn't resist
big red button.

Reached end of tether,
and swung.

———————

Searching for Venus, he found David.

———————

That day, we swapped skin colours.

———————

Self-driving car… with a grudge

———————

Breakfast club.
Naked lunch.
School dinners.

———————

Let me die in your arms.

———————

They upgraded our legs to castors.

Licked her lips, savouring his taste.

Lost: Cat.
Reward: If stays lost.

Problem gambler.
Wife bet he'd leave.

Together, they walked into the sea.

Her red flags had red flags!

You left,
and we
became me.

Sun too close.
Wax wings melted.

Roses delivered.
Same sender as recipient.

Auditioned for lead guitar.
Got tambourine.

Rival badgers see car.
Call truce.

Procured bicycle.
Rode sedately.
Died predictably.

Started a brewery.
One customer guaranteed.

Pot called the kettle. Now dating!

Our shared DNA?
Do Not Ask.

Need bigger shed.
Dragon's egg hatched!

My head is packed with lies.

No morning aches? Check your pulse.

Only twenty-four hours news left.

The new president became a queen.

Love triangle?
I'm in a dodecahedron.

Lived with cats, the pathologist noted.

Kept his eyes peeled, in jar.

Her legs spread like peanut butter.

If God exists,
he's a sociopath.

Because life's short, she said no.

8

THE FIFTH MOVEMENT

Landed.
Explored.
Adventured.
Exotic Encounters.
Devoured.

History repeats.
Mistakes made.
History repeats.

Played Russian roulette.
Landed on red.

Podiatrists love the smell of feet.

Woke up hungover.
Remembered.
Started drinking.

In the rematch,
Goliath beat David.

Finally had enough time.
Finished everything!

He learned
to love
too late.

Forget yellow snow. Avoid the brown!

For sale: Clown shoes. Never fit.

Earned ten. Spent nine.
Plus two…

Earth recovered after fish took charge.

Purchased DNA plug-ins.
Grew wings.

Drug-addled bird went cold turkey.

Chased a rainbow. Caught a munchkin.

Hand slipped into her love pocket.

Shits I passed in the night.

Drunk in car.
Dead up tree.

Celebrity chef accidentally popularised cat meat.

Even the lightning went on strike.

Danced to the cliffs.
Sighed.
Jumped.

Chances are,
your instincts are wrong.

He answered her prayers.
And left.

It's not *my* fault you're extinct.

Last thing you'll see?
My face.

Cold feet.
Warm heart.
Hot temper.

Painted the town red.
With machete.

Returned home wounded,
but dead inside.

Deny.
Fight.
Bargain.
Cry.
Never accept.

She tried.
He tried.
Both lied.

Teacher's pet uses classroom litter tray.

Superman started dating the Incredible Hulk.

Stories require a twist…
except here.

Taxidermist wanted.
Must bring own cat.

Marooned together.
Found water.
No food…

Why wait for disease? Drink antifreeze.

Next, the dead got a vote.

Made it *all* afternoon without snoozing.

All work. No play. Jack resigned.

Only her son still remembers her.

That day, his children stopped crying.

The camera lied:
I never cried.

We pickled her like an onion.

The Phrenologist felt her own head.

Undressed.
On a bed.
No memories.

9

SADNESS AND BEAUTY IN SIX WORDS

Six Word Wonders aren't all stories,
With a beginning, middle and end,
Some are just beautiful poetic thoughts.
Emotions to touch, and to send.

Your lips
are shaped
like kisses.

After fighting,
I need you more.

Delicate words drift from your lips.

I can no longer remember you.

Even poets can't
describe your eyes.

Without you,
I am barely me.

There was no music until you.

In bed.
Thinking about you,
instead.

Only through dying can we live.

Above the grey sky
is blue

When I die,
make me compost.

We danced from
dusk to daybreak.

We'll cross every new bridge together.

Whilst I babble,
you still listen.

Sleep soundly,
and dream of me.

You always zig when I zag.

My heart didn't break. It shattered.

Eight billion people.
You chose me.

10

THE SIXTH MOVEMENT

Understood the rules.
Obeyed them.
Lost.

———

Titchy Titch itched his itchy itch.

———

Used a rope.
Heard him choke.

———

Wanted: Web developer.
Preferably a spider.

Despite obvious innocence,
he pleaded guilty.

Only the king knew she lived.

She stood. He sat. Baby shat.

All same day:
Born, breathed, died.

Married young.
Now, she's forgotten me.

She's kissing another man…
Her brother.

That barber turned my hair grey.

The elephant in the room blushed.

'Left leg?'
'Right.'
The surgeon hesitated.

Madam's coffee?
Strong, black, deathly cold.

The wedding resumed, without the groom.

Made love for the last time.

The groom ballooned.
The bride cried.

His bones bent 'til they buckled.

God played dice. Threw snake eyes.

First bullied.
Now, bullies the bullies.

Female,
denied justice,
seeks caped crusader.

Eyes of saint.
Mind of sinner.

Couple never returned from their honeymoon.

Teeth sank into her bare flesh.

Wife,
ended life,
with sharp knife.

Sleeping cat?
Hasn't moved for weeks.

Wife complained.
Husband sharpened his axe.

Traded for Camel...
Doesn't even smoke.

When nightmares come,
welcome them in.

Teased wizard.
Now, I'm a goat.

Tried dirty dancing.
Made a mess.

Untie her…
I need the rope.

Wanted answers.
Learned truth.
Wanted ignorance.

That zombie wept before they fired.

Twins reunited. Both agreed - never again.

Baby said first word today.
"Oink."

New chalk board was quite re-markable.

Invisible man crouched down beside her.

Emptying herself left her much thinner.

She dropped her bags,
and left.

Positive mental attitude. Negative credit score.

Our chemistry rearranged my strongest bonds.

One clumsy tweet.
International condemnation.
Suicide.

No aftershave? Just use toilet bleach.

Murder, Mike mused, makes men monsters.

Mouse danced 'til old puss pounced.

Monday?
It's Sunday minus the hope.

Lost an arm.
Found a wristwatch.

Three hundred thousand people died yesterday.

Met boy. Slapped boy. Left boy.

11

THE SEVENTH MOVEMENT

Once upon a time… The end.

———————

Took a personality test.
Failed it.

———————

Pretty in pink. Bitch in black

———————

The turntable spun whilst I collapsed.

———————

Nailing the coffin's lid roused her.

That bull dislikes
my leather trousers.

We'll cross every new bridge together.

Hopeless romantic?
Nah. I'm just hopeless.

If it was love, I'm sorry.

"Bi-curious and curiouser," cried Alice.

Got capped teeth.
Lost all dignity.

Born.
Worked forty years.
Heart-attack.

'Whodunit?'
'Who DID it.'
'We'll see…'

So you're my granny and mommy?

Bought fool's gold.
Proved a point.

'Hell seems okay.'
'Furnace is broken.'

Found: An accountant with a personality.

Under my bed, he still waits.

'Six words?'
'Yep.'
'Not much.'
'Nope.'

Discovered her clothes on the beach.

Mini-me made massive-me muddled.

After medical school,
Simon wasn't simple.

Dumped that heartless,
selfish radiographer.
Ex-xrayer.

NASA called…
They found your wallet.

After tonight, I'll be an orphan.

'Your WIFE called,' hissed his wife.

Regrets? Not wearing a crash helmet…

In crowds,
I feel so lonely.

Clown held open door.
Nice jester.

He examined her whilst she slept.

She didn't like his "little" surprise.

Furious cheesemongers.
They went completely emmental.

Took command. Then, the fleet sank.

Licensed to kill. Prefers to chill.

Lost: One monster. Answers to Frankensteins'.

Adam wanted Eve.
Eve wanted Ella.

Gulliver developed a thing for dwarves.

'What's that?'
'Life insurance.'
'Whose?'
'Yours…'

'Wouldn't harm fly,' claims reformed spider.

'One eyeball… In exchange. Your daughter.'

Snow White got a cocaine habit.

Drank from holy grail. Tasted rusty.

Plastic surgery completed.
Got booby prize.

With you, my dreams came true.

Been shot. Just waiting to re-spawn.

'Not guilty.'
He smirked.
'Just kidding.'

How long
it takes
to suffocate...

12

THE SIX WORD WONDER ALPHABET PEOPLE

A strange bunch, all seem deranged,
These alliterative peeps really must fix,
Their peculiar lives and strange urges,
At least, they conform to six.

Angry Albert arranged another angling accident.

Boring Boris bet big - became broke.

Constipated Clara
created copious, creamy craps.

Devilish Doug decisively defeated demented
Darren.

Enviable Edgar's eccentric existence elevates
earthlings.

Fragrant Felicity's feminine features failed Frank.

Grim Gertrude
given grizzly gynaecological groping.

Hedonistic Henry hallucinated his horrific
homicide.

Ignorant Ian invented inconceivably imbecilic
irrelevances.

Joyless Jonathan just joined jealous jobless.

Kittenish Kirsty kept kaleidoscopically kinky
knowledge.

Lank Lawrence learned lengthy, libellous lessons.

Mechanical Michelle's macabre meanness meant misery.

Noble Noah - neglected naive nonbelievers notifications.

Obtuse Oprah often obviated obvious options.

Pretty Penelope,
predictably,
piled on pounds.

Quixotic Quincy queerly quacks.
Quickly quits.

Rum Rudy's raw rabid rant = racist.

Syrupy Stanley spun
saucy, selfish stories.

Towering Tatiana -
too tall to try.

Unwell Ulysses' undoing?
Urgent, unchecked ulcer.

Venereal Vince -
virulent, victimised, vaccinated, victorious.

Waggish Wilbur woke women with wink.

Xylophonist Xavier eXamined Xanthie's X-rated X-rays.

Yonder Yorick yawned; yeasty, yellowing youth.

Zany Zadie's zestful zingers zeroed Zelda's.

13

THE EIGHTH MOVEMENT

Aged forty-three. Still bottle fed.

Believe in yourself.
Somebody has to.

Wanted: Murderer who killed my inspiration.

When someone offers toothpaste.
Accept it.

She rejected him,
then ejected him.

Brontosaurus munched.
Oblivious to massive asteroid.

Secret: I'm the saddest funny person.

Nobody ever laughed
who hasn't cried.

Call an ambulance…
This'll be quick!

There is no smoke without desire.

Save paintbrushes.
Paint in the nude.

———

So much effort
being so lazy.

———

Educated to the point of ignorance.

———

You're dying from your first breath.

———

Cat,
on ninth life,
risks jump.

———

Brother skydives.
Ground breaks his fall.

———

When I die,
will you cry?

Romeo checked Juliet's ID.
Wedding's off.

Falling black box cracked my skull.

Looking for someone.
But not you.

The opposite of serendipity? This week.

Ironically,
he cheats,
whilst I iron.

Man…in the walls…is watching…

Used his eyeballs as ice cubes.

Keep calm
and don't carry on.

Why can't life just be kittens?

Listen!
The birds have stopped singing.

Hungry mammoth
forages beside
treacherous goo.

Full moon.
Rescue puppy turns werewolf.

———

Frozen vegetables make awesome ice cubes.

———

Dose of reality cured imposter syndrome.

———

If it was love,
I'm sorry.

———

Broken.
Battered.
Bruised.
But not beaten.

———

New black hole formed.
My heart.

———

World on fire - the electorate shrugged.

Virus that eventually ends us?
Mankind.

The spider's venom:
Paralysis, then calmness.

She ran slower than he walked.

Rode without stabilisers.
Walks with crutches.

Regretted kip
in bin night skip.

Santa just got convicted for trespass.

Patient patient waits for disease's return.

None of his unemployment jokes work.

Trainee wizard expelled for bad spelling.

No one even remembers the bees.

14

THE NINTH MOVEMENT

Poured out two glasses… then remembered.

Blue blood?
Wait… Where's Papa Smurf?

Bombshell
just exploded into my life.

Cheerleader. Jock. Sat together in silence.

Pancake day. Making a massive crepe.

'You pig.'
'Pig with a gun.'

'I do,' he said to him.

Comedian choked on his last joke.

He snapped the spine,
then read.

I came.
She saw.
I confessed.

After getting implants,
she felt deflated.

Alone, in bed, I hear breathing.

'Checkmate.'
'No.'
'Why?'
'We're playing badminton.'

Betty Rubble left Barney... for Wilma!

Disassembled clock.
Then reassembled.
Not ticking.

Dam burst and floodgates opened. Stalemate.

Believed in ghosts. Died. Stopped believing.

———

Chose toad over
evening with Prince.

———

Dunk bathed his body in tea.

———

Emergency services
listened to him die.

———

German food is undoubtedly the wurst.

———

Found trapper:
Caught in bear trap.

———

Gorgeous on the outside.
Inside?
Spaghetti.

***

Kept the box she came in.

***

Her father's
her half-sister's son.

***

The reflection slowly blinked.
She didn't.

***

Burglar apologises,
but gun already fired.

***

His final cigarette was the longest.

***

Got his immigration papers.
She emigrated.

He discovered unsolvable conundrum.
Married her.

My tragic downfall?
Replied to all.

Hit the male on the head.

Hoarder cured!
Now she collects minimalists.

How cold
she became
by morning.

Kicked his head.
Now, he's dead.

When you smiled,
my heart stopped.

He taught her love then hate.

Aliens came and went.
Nobody noticed.

Life ended
when she said no.

Murder weapon?
A sharpened red herring.

Left arm chopped off.
Alright now...

The old king died.
Nobody cried.

Love magnets.
One attracts.
One resists.

Scientists discover another newly-extinct species.

My life is laundry.
Rinsed.
Repeat.

Newborn,
immediately,
received an unwanted inheritance.

Nobody understands why I love you.

She's never casual
with her discipline.

Bumped into my nemesis. Nice guy.

15

DO JOKES WORK IN SIX WORDS?

Do jokes work in six words?
It's true: Not every one's funny.
But, occasional nouns coupled with verbs
Turn out to be quite punny.

Sued the airline.
Lost my case.

Stole her diary.
Got twelve months.

He wouldn't share the oysters.
Shellfish.

Joined a rubber bank.
Check bounced.

The religious fishmongers believed in cod.

Evil criminal tripped on curb.
Felon.

Buying another lizard. I'm scaling up.

Schoolboy sneaking a quick doze.
Kidnapping.

Last night, Warren pulled a rabbit.

Busy librarian was unavailable.
Booked up.

Unforgettably intense camping trip - in tents.

Typical!
Hotel California is fully booked.

'Able seaman.'
'Great… And your occupation?'

———

Gave that AA meeting full marks.

———

After the car crash,
the autopsy.

———

Met any acupuncturists?
They're all pricks.

———

'Heard about the indecisive bee?'
'Maybe.'

———

His sabre rattled.
Damn Jedi technology.

———

I'm buying a stairlift to heaven.

Time travel is possible…
Just wait!

Without you, there'd be no YouTube.

16

THE TENTH MOVEMENT

Admitted male.
Paperwork mishap.
Left female.

———

For Dave,
it's a no-brainer.

———

Found: A Colt Revolver. Still warm.

———

Forced to cancel her maternity leave.

Cupid.
Tomorrow, aim for his head.

Counted chickens.
None hatched.
Stupid sayings.

Last to call
the first responders.

Burnt flesh
peeled like an orange.

Lost condom. Extra large. He wasn't.

Busking bagpiper executed.
Cruel, but inevitable.

'What are my treatment options?'
'...Hope...?'

'Virgin no longer,' the stranger whispered.

'I will destroy this planet.'
'...Mum?'

Yesterday,
she jumped off the bandwagon.

Valentine's card.
Recognised the handwriting.
Mine.

Tide rolled out.
Tsunami rolled in.

Wrinkle-resistant skin.
Roll your own.

You'll keep living until you're alone.

Ken started wearing
Barbie's favourite dress.

Always check behind closed shower curtains.

Belly-flopped into pool.
Emptied it.

Thumbelina and Tom Thumb
declare war!

…chicken came before egg came before…

Through the reinforced glass,
you apologised.

Beautiful twin daughters:
Kate and DupliKate.

New house:
Two floors.
Multiple flaws.

They died together, hand in hand.

The master rose up,
and tap-danced.

Fly flew over the spider's spies.

Still wondering
if you ever existed.

The lampshade turned and kissed him.

His dreams came true…
Sorry…
Nightmares!

Now you're here,
I can feed.

Forgot the alphabet.
Don't know why.

'I banged her,' bragged the universe.

Actor plays characters,
but has none.

The backward cheesemakers made edam.

Live,
and let everyone else die.

Award-winning gastropub
serves only gastropods.

My ultimate failure was your success.

Lazy worm outwitted the early bird.

Swam through my pool of tears.

The killer
grinned
at the accused.

Her lips were red.
Blood red.

The final meal was
his tongue.

Unloved celebrity bought gun.
Shooting star.

Stone hearted.
Ice tempered.
Brittle boned.

Her hair had just grown back.

And they lived happily ever after…

SO, YOU'RE NEAR THE FINAL PAGE

So, you're near the final page,
Made it through the danger-zone,
Perhaps, you're asking, 'So what's next?'
Easy: now you write your own.

Grab a pen, keyboard or crayon,
Or one of those new thingamajigs,
Get creative, get busy, get composing,
Keep stories short, but ideas big.

SIX REASONS TO WRITE SIX WORDS

Therapy - writing is soothing and mindful.

Craft - tight stories need authorial skill.

Practicing brevity - keeping it simple, stupid.

Refining arguments - reword until it's perfect.

Core language skills - dictionary, thesaurus, research.

Health - we're all addicted to passivity.

ADVICE FOR ASPIRING SIX WORD WONDERS

Here are a few friendly pointers,
To let your creative juice flow.
Anyone can write six word wonders,
I know this because I know.

Each wonder consists of **six words**.

Use **punctuation** to enhance your meaning.

Aim for **beginning, middle and end**.

Spark an emotion, suspense or surprise.

Many stories benefit from **a twist.**

Like a joke, **punchlines are welcome.**

Strong verbs produce much stronger stories.

Mould ideas until the shape fits.

Share your work - **listen to feedback.**

Titles are included in word count.

Contractions allowed: It's for it is.

Hyphenated-words count as **two words.**

Have fun - rules can be broken.

20

THIS IS THE END, MY FRIEND

That's it. The end. No more.
All hail the Six Word Wonder.
Whether you loathe them, or adore,
Let no one put 'em asunder.

Now, if you've time, there's Amazon:
Add a review, if you're willing.
Why not share your creations online?
Birthing a sixer is quite thrilling.

Want more stories?
We're at www.dougweller.net/six

Find new stories on
Instagram: @sixwordwonder

Final thought, till next we meet:

Enjoy your life. There's no repeat.

ACKNOWLEDGMENTS

This book is a product of the 2020 lockdown. Although I have been writing these miniature stories for many years, it took a global pandemic for me to sit down and get them into some kind of order. My thoughts are with everyone affected by the tragedy of Covid-19.

I'd like to thank my readers, especially Kirsty Langsdale and Duncan Forsyth - your feedback and thoughts are, as ever, hugely appreciated. Also, thanks to all my beta readers - Meghbhowmik, Kjkennedy, Beenareads, Emilieknight, Dragonet07 and to my generous advance readers.

If you as a reader are interested in being a beta reader or receive an advance reader copy for future books, the simply join the mailing list at dougweller.net.

My cover design is by Monandmon.

It is said that Hemmingway originated the Six Word form, although many say that's merely a myth. Either way, he was a master of brevity, so I give thanks to his name popularising the form.

Lastly, I'd like to thank everyone who follows Six Word Wonder on Instagram @sixwordwonder. Your comments and feedback provide me with the inspiration and energy to keep on writing.

Printed in Poland
by Amazon Fulfillment
Poland Sp. z o.o., Wrocław